High Seas

Hijack

A John Deacon Action Adventure

Mike Boshier

Published by Okoromai Bay Ltd.

1

Even his wraparound sunglasses couldn't keep the sand being churned up by the rhythmic 'whump whump whump' of the slowly spinning rotor blades out of his eyes. Pulling his protective goggles in place, Deacon gave the thumbs up to the loadmaster who slid the side door closed and turned and tapped the pilot twice on the shoulder. As the whine of the turbines increased, Deacon and his men pulled ear defenders over their ears, as the whump of the blades became all-encompassing and the outside view dissolved into a sandy dust storm. With a lurch, the twin-engine Sea Hawk helicopter rose rapidly into the sky before dipping its nose and heading north across the airfield, as Acting Lieutenant John Deacon, along with Bryant Schaefer, Bill Hymann and Ernesto Swarez of SEAL team Bravo, lifted off from Camp Lemonnier, in Djibouti, on their sixth mission in as many weeks.

The United States Naval Expeditionary Base, situated at Djibouti's Djibouti–Ambouli International Airport, was and still is, the only permanent US military base in Africa, and is home to the Combined Joint Task Force - Horn of Africa (CJTF-HOA) of the U.S. Africa Command (USAFRICOM).

With all navigation lights out and keeping to a flying altitude of only 100 feet, within moments the helicopter was invisible as it flew northeast heading towards Perim Island, Yemen, over the Gulf of Tadjoura, leaving Moucha Island close to port. Thirty minutes of flying time would bring them over the rocky outcrop islands collectively known as the 7 Brothers before they would approach the twenty-mile-wide, eighty-mile-long Bab al-Mandab Strait separating the Yemen and Djibouti shipping lanes.

Ships heading from Europe to Asia pass south through the Suez Canal before entering the northern portion of the Red Sea, running north-west to south-east. Egypt, Sudan, Eritrea and

Djibouti borders its western banks, with Egypt, Saudi Arabia and Yemen bordering its eastern. Much of the area is extremely shallow and, close to the Bab al-Mandab Straits, the depth of water of 50 meters or more is limited to a channel of only 7 miles width. There are also numerous rocks and shallows all waiting to ground and sink an unwary mariner. Once through the Strait, the Gulf of Aden opens east to west with depths between 1,000 and 2,000 metres starting at the Tadjoura Trough, with the only remaining shipping hazards being the islands of Abd al Kuri, Samhah, Darsah and Socotra at its eastern end, islands now owned and operated by the government of Yemen. For centuries, this 'easy-picking' area from the Red Sea to the island of Socotra has been home to pirates and adventurers, including the fabled 'Sinbad'.

Nowadays ships heading eastwards towards the rich, populous cities in the Persian Gulf and Asia stay slightly north of the mid-channel until clear of Socotra. Once passed, those heading into the Persian Gulf via the Gulf of Oman keep further north, while ships heading towards India and Asia head south-east to clear the tips of Sri Lanka and India. Lookouts at the radar stations on the 1,000-metre-high central island mountain have unobstructed views of vessels transiting these areas, and regularly transmit their findings to colleagues in Yemen and Somalia.

2

With a change of engine note, the helicopter altered course slightly and began its final approach to a particular ship travelling south from the Red Sea. This large container ship, the *MV Oklahoma*, was en route from the U.S. via Europe to Malaysia. Flying the Stars and Stripes, it was U.S.-flagged, meaning it was American owned and registered in the U.S. and subject to U.S. laws and protection.

The pilot skillfully banked the helicopter and carefully hovered over the empty stern section, matching his sideways speed with the forward motion of the *Oklahoma*. It was dangerous work - a small error and the tips of the rotor blades would hit the containers, shattering immediately and dropping the helicopter into the maelstrom of white water at the stern. Although clear of the propellers, the churning water would suck anything landing in it down to the depths. With sweat forming on his brow and his hands constantly altering the sideways drift and speed of his machine, the pilot matched it perfectly with the speed of the ship. With the side door already opened, the loadmaster kicked four two-inch thick rappelling lines out, two from each side of the 'copter. As they unravelled like snakes darting down towards the ship, Deacon and his men, all wearing thick, protective leather gloves, quickly grasped the lines and rappelled down them, one man per line. Each man was also carrying two large holdall bags. Within seconds of them clearing, the helicopter loadmaster began retrieving the lines before they could become wrapped around anything or trapped, which would bring certain death to the 'copter hovering above. As he secured the last line, he commanded the pilot to pull away, and the helicopter gently rose clear of harm's way before turning and heading back towards Camp Lemonnier.

Lt. Deacon and Schaefer carried their holdalls towards the ship's superstructure before climbing the stairs towards the bridge, leaving the other men below. Entering, Deacon said, "Captain! Lt. Deacon and Schaefer reporting."

Piracy in and around the Gulf of Aden, the Arabian Sea and near the coast of Somalia had started in earnest since 2005. In 1991, the civil war in Somalia brought down the previous government. After that time and with no effective coastguard maintaining government control of the 2,000-mile coastline, racketeers moved in. Initially, fishing fleets from around the world, all flying flags of convenience, moved in and plundered the area. In 2005, a United Nations report estimated over $300 million of fish and seafood was being stolen each year from the Somalian rightful owners. For centuries, the Horn of Africa region has been seen as 'easy pickings'. Only ten-percent of roads in Somalia are paved, most being just dirt tracks, making transportation and even communication poor. Most Somalians living on or near the coast were simple fisherman just trying to eke out a living. With the advent of the rogue fishing fleets and their use of intensive fishing methods, including undersized nets, the local fishermen's method of making a paltry living were compromised. Initially, some found compensation by seizing the illegal fishing boats, whose owners and operators would quickly pay small ransoms in return for not drawing attention to their violation of international maritime law.

To make matters worse, foreign ships were often spotted dumping toxic waste off the coast. A 2005 United Nations Environmental Program report cited the dumping of radioactive and other hazardous deposits in the Somalian waters. According to the U.N., at the time of the report, it cost $2.50 per tonne for a European company to dump these types of materials off the Horn of Africa, as opposed to $250 per tonne to dispose of them cleanly in Europe.

That year, four large ships, including a luxury cruise liner, were attacked, three of them successfully, with millions of dollars being paid in ransom. During

2006, the attacks slowed against civilian ships, but the *USS Cape St. George* and *USS Gonzalez*, both U.S. Naval vessels, were fired on by pirates. In 2007, there were eight successful hijackings. During 2008 it increased to over fifty, approximately one per week, and rose again in 2009 to seventy-six. In April, the *MV Maersk Alabama*, the first U.S.-flagged and owned ship was captured. This particular hijacking became world famous when the four pirates released the crew but detained the captain, Richard Phillips, and the five of them travelled towards Somalia in one of the *Alabama's* stolen powered lifeboats. Due to public pressure, the U.S. President unleashed the Navy and the destroyer

USS Bainbridge, frigate *USS Halyburton*, and amphibious assault ship *USS Boxer* were dispatched to the Gulf of Aden in response to the hostage situation. On April 10th, six members of SEAL Team Six flew from Oceana, Virginia, direct to the Somalia coast. Their Air Force C-17 cargo plane refuelled in the air no fewer than three times during the 16-hour flight. The operation was planned so that they would parachute into the ocean under cover of darkness, before being picked up by colleagues on the *USS Boxer*. Two days later, SEAL sniper teams killed three hijackers and rescued Captain Richard Phillips alive, with one hijacker being arrested.

Now in early 2010 hijackings hadn't stopped with many vessels being taken. The hijacked ships were usually anchored close inshore, with the crews taken off and held hostage ashore under armed guard with orders to kill the hostages in the event of any rescue attempt. Shipping owners had no choice but to pay, and millions of dollars in ransoms were being paid monthly. Some western countries started placing their warships in and around the area to try to ward off the attackers, but many of the pirates were desperate, and hijackings continued. Any pirates captured were held and released over to the Somalian Government but were usually released soon after, ready to return and try again.

The last time international piracy of ships had been a problem was back in the 1700 and 1800s in the days of sailing ships. Then pirates caught would be tried, found guilty, and executed by hanging. However, in today's PC conscious world and with the issue of International Human Rights to contend with, this was no longer acceptable.

However, the U.S. President wanted action and wanted it quickly. Realising any involvement by U.S. Forces would need to be kept secret, he authorised the placement of small contingents of U.S. SEALs on approved U.S.-flagged vessels transiting the area, with orders to use deadly force if necessary. But only ships where the owners and crew were willing to sign the Espionage Act of 1917, a poorly worded U.S. basic version equivalent of the UK's Official Secrets Act.

Other countries and nations took many more months before deciding whether to place armed guards on their flagged vessels, including the UK.

After introducing themselves to the captain and first officer, Deacon explained his orders.

"Sir, we are to protect the *Oklahoma* at whatever cost is necessary. There will be four of us on board, two on duty at any time. Our mission is to deter attack. We are authorised to use deadly force if necessary, but only as a last resort. The nature of this mission is secret hence the reason your company requested you each sign the Espionage Act. I would appreciate if you could inform the crew that we are on board and provide us with keys and access throughout the ship."

"How long do you expect to be on board?" the captain asked, nodding.

"At this stage, Captain, 5 days as that will cover you from Djibouti to somewhere off the Maldives where we will be picked up by our colleagues. What's your planned speed?"

"The company like us to conserve fuel whenever we can, Lieutenant, so we are cruising at 16 knots. Our maximum continual speed is 23, but we use far more fuel, almost 45% more. However, the company has authorised me to push to 23 knots in the event of an attack and to continue at that speed until approximately 400 miles south-east of Socotra, then back to 16."

3

For the next two days, it was business as usual for the crew. Although the captain had announced they were on board, most of the crew kept away and just busied themselves with their regular tasks. Deacon and his men had examined the ship in detail looking for the easiest areas the hijackers would likely attack from and the best firing angles to deter them. Usually, pirates attack ships from the rear coming up close behind and using ladders or grappling hooks to climb near the stern. Human nature being what it is, most people look forward, and lookouts are usually placed looking forward and to the sides of the ship. Very rarely do non-military people bother looking behind them. Even at sea, an overtaking vessel is expected to keep clear of the craft it is overtaking, so it is only with the advent of radar showing a 360-degree picture that the area behind a travelling ship is often observed. The second most popular way to gain access to a ship was via the sides. Heavily laden ships lie low in the water, and if the attackers could get in close, the height of the deck from the sea is much less, meaning a shorter and quicker climb by ladder or rope.

The crew also spotted the SEALs attaching what looked to be rolled-up banners to some of the containers on the port and starboard sides. Early on the third morning, with Schaefer and Hyman on duty and Deacon and Swarez asleep, the first mate called the captain to inform him that radar had picked up two small fast-moving skiff-type craft following them. They were too far away in the dark to see, but radar showed them approaching at 35 knots and closing the distance fast. Grabbing the phone handset to the engine room, the captain shouted, "We are under attack. This is not a drill. I want maximum speed. Remove the rev limits."

The senior engineer obeyed at once, first removing the engine revolutions per minute limits, and then pushing the manual throttles to their stops. The engines slowly began to increase speed over the next four minutes until they were running flat out, producing a little over 24 knots. The senior engineer didn't think he could maintain those revolutions indefinitely, but certainly for the next hour or two. Schaffer had also gone to wake up Deacon, but the change in the rhythm of the engine had already alerted him. Deacon and Swarez were up and ready. Checking the radar screen again, Deacon estimated it would take the chasing skiffs almost 45 minutes to overhaul them. He ordered the banners unravelled, anti-hijacking hoses primed and his men to get in place. The captain also had a plan of action to follow and pressed the emergency button on the

Tannoy system. Picking up the handset he waited until the klaxon had sounded three times before stating clearly 'Charlie, Charlie, Charlie - this is not a drill. Charlie, Charlie, Charlie - this is not a drill' over the loudspeakers, putting all 15 of his crew on full alert. 'Charlie Charlie Charlie' was the code signal adopted some years previously by Royal Caribbean ships, and has since been adopted by many other shipping companies, meaning 'Security Threat'.

Moving to the satellite radio system, he was about to radio for assistance to the impending attack when Deacon stopped him.

"Captain, with us on board there is no need to raise the alarm elsewhere. Just keep control of the ship and do as I say."

With the rise in hijackings over the last few years, many ships transiting the area had been fitted with a variety of anti-hijacking measures, including locked gates and railings across access points along the ship, along with high-pressure water cannons to flood attacking vessels and disable individuals. Later defences would be added to also include LRAD Long Range Acoustic Devices to beam high-frequency high-powered sound beams to induce pain and disorientation in any attackers; electrified razor wire located along the top of side rails to hamper climbers; as well as non-lethal lasers, used to temporarily blind attackers from up to a 1-mile distance.

The *Oklahoma* was fitted with gates and water cannons, and after getting Deacon's agreement, the captain ordered the water cannons activated and all non-essential doors and access gates to be locked. Deacon and his men unravelled the two banners they'd fitted previously, one along each side of the ship clearly displaying in English and Somali, the official language of Somalia, 'This ship is protected. Any attack will be met with deadly force.'

In the meantime, Bill Hymann had switched on a radio jamming system, which blocked all marine frequency transmissions in the standard 156 - 162

MHz bands, while continually playing a message in English and Somali on channel 16 - the International Distress Frequency, at low power the same message as displayed on the banners. This radio transmission stopped all other marine communications, apart from the receiving of the outgoing statement on channel 16, to all vessels within a five-mile radius of the ship and also had the added benefit of stopping the pirates communicating with each other or to their support ship. Although officially in breach of international rules set by the International Telecommunications Union, and the International Maritime Organisation of which the USA is a member to the misuse of international maritime frequencies, the view of the US Government was this was a small price to pay if a hijacking could be averted.

As the attacking craft drew closer, travelling quickly along the relatively smooth wake caused by the hull and powerful engines of the *Oklahoma*, Deacon stationed Hymann and Swarez on either side of the ship a dozen or so yards forward of the rear superstructure. This provided them with the best firing position if the pirates tried to pull alongside. Bryant Schaefer was stationed on the rear deck near the stern mast to give a good cross-fire angle, and Deacon himself remained on the through-bridge thereby allowing quick access to either side of the ship.

As the pair of chasing craft approached the rear of the *Oklahoma*, Deacon could see five people in each skiff, made up of one steering and four holding weapons. As they neared, they split formation to approach both sides of the *Oklahoma* simultaneously. From his vantage point, Schaefer fired the first shots at their outboard engines. He was the best marksman on board, and even at four hundred yards distance the clang of his rounds hitting the metal casings could be heard above the noise of the wind and whine of their outboard engines.

"Captain, please turn 15 degrees to port," Deacon requested.

Although large, the ship responded quickly to changes in direction and as she turned, the chasing craft heading for her port side also had to turn to save running into her stern. In doing so, she left the relative smooth comfort of the *Oklahoma's* wake and was tossed about in the sea's waves. Coupled with the increase in speed of the *Oklahoma*, the chasing craft had a hard time trying to keep up. As it cleared the wave tops and became almost airborne, Schaefer's rounds began to hit home, and two fired in quick succession hit the starboard outboard engine cowling and gearbox. With wisps of dark smoke beginning to rise from the engine and the scream of metal as the gears chewed on the full-metal-jacket rounds, the pirate steering the craft had no choice other than to slow down, soon becoming lost to sight in the choppy sea. Deacon ordered the captain to change course to starboard by 30 degrees to try to use the same technique against the second craft. However, this pirate was more experienced than his colleague and had already pulled further starboard. Although he had to slow his speed due to the size of the waves, the turning to starboard of the *Oklahoma* actually closed the distance between the two craft quickly. The starboard skiff was by now too far ahead for Schaefer to get a close firing angle on it, so Ernesto Swarez, located a little further forward on the starboard side took up the challenge. As the skiff approached the starboard side of the *Oklahoma*, Swarez began firing carefully along the lower part of the craft's hull. Each shot hit home and had the desired effect of making the attackers huddle down below the side coaming. Although three of them raised their weapons and fired in the general direction of where Swarez was hiding, and although a few shots had come close, none caused him any harm with most merely ricocheting off the metal of the containers.

Stood on the bridge, Deacon had a bird's eye view and could see one pirate manhandling an RPG. He spoke over the private radio comms system for Swarez to hurry up and take the engines out just as one of Swarez's rounds hit the port engine. With fuel spraying out of a fractured line it ignited, with flames spreading over the stern. The pirate with the RPG was moving the aim towards the Oklahoma when Deacon ordered Swarez to take the shot. Two rounds hit the pirate's chest, and he fell back as the RPG fired harmlessly into the sky.

With both chase skiffs disabled, and one of them on fire, the *Oklahoma* rapidly drew away and out of range. Continuing on at 24 knots she quickly began to disappear towards the horizon, leaving the Pirates to call for help from their support boat once they were out of range of the radio jamming system.

4

After the excitement of the previous hour, the crew returned to their standard duties, and the captain reduced speed back to 16 knots while Deacon and his team kept a close watch on the radar. However, he believed the chances of them being attacked again were extremely slim, and the rest of the trip was uneventful.

Two days later, when approaching the middle of the Arabian Sea and outside the range of the Somalian pirates, a US Navy Sea Hawk picked the SEALs up from the *Oklahoma*. The pilot approached slowly and hovered overhead before delicately lowering until approximately three feet above the central stack of forty-foot metal containers. Deacon and his colleagues had already climbed on top of the containers along with all their gear. With the skill gained from hundreds of hours of flying, the pilot kept the Sea Hawk hovering and moving in perfect time with the *MV Oklahoma*. Under the buffeting downdraft, Deacon and his men quickly loaded their holdalls back into the helicopter before climbing aboard themselves. With a final wave from the SEALs the Sea Hawk rose and moved rapidly off to the starboard side, the ship's captain giving two blasts of the ship's horn in thanks, before the Sea Hawk returned to the *USS Harry S. Truman*, kingpin of the Fifth Fleet Carrier Battle Group steaming through the Arabian Sea. The following day the SEALs were back on duty, and the four were dropped onto another U.S.-flagged Europe and America bound container ship out of Hong Kong. This north-west bound ship travelled slightly quicker, and its journey was completely uneventful. Four-and-half days later Deacon and his team were picked up in the same manner by helicopter just off the coast of Djibouti and returned to Camp Lemonnier.

The Republic of Djibouti is located in the west of the Horn of Africa, at the southern end of the Red Sea with a population of almost 1 million of which ninety percent are of Muslim faith. It is strategically located near some of the world's busiest shipping lanes controlling access to the Red Sea and the Indian Ocean. The U.S. Navy was by far the largest employer in the region, and all Navy personnel lived permanently on the base. The main problem with Camp Lemmonier, Deacon thought, was the lack of things to do when not on duty. Going into Djibouti town itself was possible, but most of the locals didn't like Americans. They wouldn't usually cause trouble, but you could feel a palpable tension in the air. Many supported Osama bin Laden, and Al-Qaeda were becoming dominant across the water in Yemen. In fact, Al-Qaeda in the Arabian Peninsula (AQAP) was to become a union of Al-Qaeda's branches in Saudi Arabia and Yemen.

Surprisingly, the U.S. Government had realised how basic the region was and had provided as best it could at the base. There were baseball squares, a tennis court, a running track, a cinema, a couple of fast-food outlets, and of course the beach. There were kayaks and dinghies as well as two motorboats for water-skiing. SEALs are as much at home in the water as on land, and every chance he could Deacon would practice swimming, usually competing against his best friend, Bryant Schaefer, for a dollar or two each race. They'd joined the Navy together, gone through BUDs training on the same team, and completed numerous successful missions together. Deacon had been promoted faster than Bryant, but they'd become and still remained close friends.

Up until the last mission, Deacon had been a Lieutenant Junior Grade O2 under the leader of Bravo team B at Camp Lemonnier, Lt Commander Robert Dixon. Unfortunately, after complaining of grumbling stomach pains for much of the day, Robert Dixon had suddenly started severe vomiting as his appendix ruptured and split, and he was rushed into surgery before being airlifted to Ramstein Airbase in Germany to recuperate, home of one of the largest

U.S. military hospitals outside mainland USA.

Deacon had immediately been promoted to Acting Full Lieutenant O3 and assumed full responsibility for SEAL team B at Camp Lemonnier.

5

The *Arabian Star*, a Panama-registered oil tanker out of Kuwait en route to Milford Haven, UK, was running slightly late. Tied up to loading platform 'C' in Port Mina al-Ahmadi in Kuwait, and connected by three 16 inch diameter flexible pipes each pumping 75,000 barrels of oil per hour it would usually take just under nine hours to fill her cavernous tanks.

However, a technical delay had reduced its filling capacity. One of the multiple pumps filling it was failing and running at a slower speed meaning it took eight hours longer than expected to fill the carrier to its 2 million barrels of light sweet crude, or 84 million gallons' capacity aboard the 400 metre gargantuan. Eager to make up lost time, the captain was keen to get underway as soon as possible. He had planned the trip back to Suez in close company to two container ships, as rarely have pirates attacked one ship within a group; lone ships being easier targets. However, the delay in filling meant he had to get underway as soon as possible to make up lost time.

Use of conventional radios and cell phones are banned in and around the oil and gas terminals and on board oil and gas tankers because of the risk of fire and explosion. Instead, workers must use specialised equipment designed and classified as 'Intrinsically Safe', or IS, for use in these hostile environments. As the *Arabian Star* finally dropped her mooring ropes and was manhandled out of her berth by two powerful tugboats, fussing like a mother sending her child off to school, a terminal dockworker lifted his specialised radio from his belt, changed frequencies to a specific channel and radioed that the *Arabian Star* was now underway. Switching his radio back to the primary channel he clipped it back on his belt having only been 'off network' for less than a minute.

In a tiny darkened interior room within a nondescript building in the crowded suburb of Fahaheel between

Mina al-Ahmadi and Kuwait City, an operator sat waiting. Quickly jotting down the details the operator blipped the radio once to confirm receipt of the message before turning to his computer screen. Five minutes after the radio message was heard an encrypted email was sent.

Similar to aircraft where flight durations can be calculated down to within a few minutes leeway before an aeroplane even leaves the ground, international shipping relies on consistent speed and timing of vessels from port to port. Even a small delay can have a large knock-on effect of berthing costs, and captains are encouraged to make up any time lost, bearing in mind their other challenge of conserving fuel usage. Therefore, a captain will authorise a small increase in speed over a longer period to regain time, versus a quicker approach that would burn excessive fuel. With set waypoints of ships courses in the heavily trafficked Persian Gulf, Gulf of Oman and Gulf of Aden already known, along with the choke points of the Straits of Hormuz and Bab al-Mandab, and the speed limitations within these areas, the captain merely requested the onboard computer to recalculate. It took only moments for the new time-to-waypoint (TTW) timings for the *Arabian Star* from Mina al-Ahmadi oil terminal all the way to the entry lock at the southern end of the

Suez Canal to be calculated and displayed.

Unfortunately, the same people in Yemen and Somalia receiving messages from the lookouts on Socotra Island and the informer in Fahaheel also operated the same sophisticated software. As soon as the email message of the delayed departure of the *Arabian Star* had been received, they had also recalculated the TTW's of all the known and expected waypoints the *Arabian Star* would transit.

Early in the morning of the fourth day just after the crew had changed watch two skiffs managed to get alongside undiscovered, and the *Arabian Star* was hijacked off the coast of Salahal, Oman, before being diverted south towards southern Somalia. The crew were taken entirely by surprise; the first the captain knew being two armed hijackers bursting onto the bridge waving loaded Kalashnikovs in his face. Once the company's headquarters had been informed news quickly spread of the successful hijacking and press estimated the expected ransom for a ship of this size and cargo to be almost £200 million.

Once alerted to the hijacking, the UK Government immediately asked if the U.S. had anyone nearby who could offer assistance. Deacon and his team were back at Camp Lemonnier and not due to be placed aboard any other U.S.-flagged ships for another forty-eight hours.

Trained to intercept and board ships travelling at speed at sea, they were ordered to prepare to retake the Arabian Star as quickly as possible. Speed was essential as after the ship reached its final destination the crew would be removed and held under armed guard ashore. Any rescue attempt at that stage would likely result in large numbers of casualties.

6

The Lockheed C-130 took off from Djibouti with Deacon and his men on board and headed east by south-east over the Horn of Africa. By now the tanker was forty miles off the coast near Bandarbeyla and still heading towards its expected destination of Garacad, Mudug, an isolated fishing port halfway down the coast towards Mogadishu. This entire area of Somalia was 'bandit territory' and under the rule of various drug lords whose word was law. Conventional law and order hadn't existed here for over a dozen years, and even the Somali Army were hesitant about operating in the area.

It took the C-130 over ninety minutes to travel the 580 miles distance, and it was by now a little after 04:30 am the morning following the hijack. From seventeen thousand feet altitude, the *Arabian Star* looked tiny against the inky black of the ocean. Running with just regular navigation lights showing, she was hard to make out from above without the use of night vision goggles. The pilot banked and placed his aircraft eight miles upwind of the ship far below, and the four SEALs of team B exited the rear ramp on cue. As their darkened parachutes opened automatically, Deacon steered them towards the ship far below. Split into two pairs the SEALs approached the dark tanker from both sides. Ernesto Swarez came in too fast from the starboard side and misjudged the angle of the pipe-derrick in the dark. Trying to turn level with the direction the ship was heading he was hit by a sudden upsurge draft partly collapsing his chute and slamming him into the derrick, breaking his arm and dislocating his shoulder. The other three landed safely completely undetected and quickly set about checking their comrade before quietly approaching the bridge superstructure. Deacon didn't know how many pirates were on board but estimated it to be between six and ten based on previous hijackings and that there were two boarding ladders still attached to the railings. It looked like they had managed to get a large skiff alongside the smooth metal side of the tanker undetected and had raised the ladders up over the long side edge of the ship, known as a gunwale. The fact the tanker was full of crude oil and lying very low in the water had greatly aided their attack. Deacon would discover later the pirates were armed only with Kalashnikov rifles and had quickly stormed the bridge overpowered and beaten the unarmed crew, before locking all but the captain and first officer down below.

With his broken arm in a sling, but still able to shoot straight, Swarez was positioned in the shadows by the bridge superstructure entrance to stand guard, while the three remaining team members quietly entered and moved along the corridors. Rounding the corner of the first-floor corridor Deacon came to a Somalian sat outside a closed door, smoking with his Kalashnikov leaning against the wall. Firing a three-shot burst directly into his chest from his suppressed M4A1 assault rifle before the surprised guard could raise the alarm, he slumped and slid off the chair onto the floor, leaving a red trail of blood on the wall behind him as his cigarette dropped to the floor. Smiling, Deacon murmured, "Didn't your mother ever tell you smoking is bad for you," as he crushed it out under his soft canvas boot. With Hymann and Schaefer guarding either end of the corridor, Deacon gently opened the door to see the eager faces of the crew staring back at him.

Confirming there was no other guard within the room, and after double-checking the number of pirates on board and the whereabouts of the captain and first officer, he told the crew to stay where they were.

As the three of them slowly approached the bridge they could see two men wearing t-shirts and sandals stood outside and smoking. Two pairs of two suppressed shots each and both locals were down, although one of the pirates dropped his rifle as he fell which hit the deck with a clang. Moments later, the port door to the bridge opened, and a head leant out while something was said in Somali. Two suppressed shots from Schaefer blew the hijacker's head apart, brains and grey matter spraying back into the bridge. As the pirate died, his finger tightened on the trigger and his Kalashnikov starting spraying rounds against the superstructure, sparks dancing off in all directions, but within seconds it was all over. Moments after Schaefer had fired, Deacon and Hyman raced in through the starboard bridge door quickly sighting and firing on the two remaining hijackers. Both went down without even raising their weapons, and within a few moments the captain and first officer were shaking hands and thanking the SEALs. After confirming there had only been six pirates on board and all were accounted for, Deacon turned to the captain, saluted and said, "The ship, Captain, is yours." Swarez released the prisoners and joined them on the bridge, and they began to relax, joking at the irony of a bunch of pirates smoking cigarettes while floating on a man-made bomb carrying millions of gallons of highly volatile explosive crude oil. Deacon laughed as he said, "See guys, that's why you shouldn't smoke." Within the hour the bodies had been photographed and fingerprinted before being placed in body bags, and the *Arabian Star* had been turned around and was now back on course for Suez and the UK. It took almost 48 hours to get back to Djibouti and Deacon and his team spent the time between guarding the ship and enjoying its comforts, including comfortable beds, the latest movies and even a small plunge swimming pool. After what seemed far too short a break, they were again being dropped off, along with the corpses to a waiting launch, as they passed Djibouti.

That should have been the end of the matter. However, the crew were given extended leave after arriving in Milford Haven, and the story quickly spread in the bars and nightclubs concerning what had happened. Once it hit social media the story went viral, and within a day or

so both the British and U.S. Govern-
ments were issuing 'No comment'
replies.

Unfortunately, the story of the night
time parachuting onto the darkened deck
of a large oil tanker by special forces
didn't go unnoticed.

7

Deacon and his team, along with SEAL team A, spent the next three weeks protecting various U.S.-flagged vessels. No other hijackings occurred, and the day-to-day routine became mundane. Swarez's shoulder had been reset, and his broken Ulna had healed well. He was still not yet fit for duty and had returned to Coronado headquarters where he was currently stationed in Support and Administration, much to his annoyance. Declan 'Flan' O'Flannigan, an Irish American from Boston had joined Deacon's team while Swarez was recuperating. All SEALs are trained to the same incredibly high standards, and O'Flannigan quickly settled in.

The *Methane Queen*, a 225m Liquid Natural Gas Tanker, was full just awaiting paperwork signoff. Currently berthed in the massive Ras Laffan LNG Terminal in Qatar, the *Methane Queen* has a capacity of almost 3 billion cubic feet of methane gas. Chilled to minus 260 degrees, a temperature that transforms the gas from a vapour to a liquid, the methane is also compressed to a ratio of 600 to 1, making it economical to transport around the world. The *Methane Queen*, along with other large LNG carriers are basically giant pressurised thermos containers. They are also seen as floating bombs, each with the explosive power of a small nuclear device.

Setting sail early the following morning, the *Methane Queen* began her long voyage south down through the Arabian Sea to the Indian Ocean, before rounding the Cape of Good Hope into the South Atlantic, and heading north-west up towards the Gulf of Mexico and her final destination at the Sabine Pass LNG Terminal in Louisiana. Due to her size and her cargo, she was unable to transit the Suez Canal; hence the long journey around the tip of Africa.

Unfortunately for the U.S. Government in enacting the President's Executive Order, a simple clerical error had only identified ships needing protection as those transiting the Gulf of Aden. This small error meant the *Methane Queen*, along with numerous other ships heading south from the Persian Gulf towards the Cape of Good Hope, had not been identified as possible hijack risks.

Her journey through the Persian Gulf and around the Straits of Hormuz was uneventful. Painted bright red and with large white lettering of LNG on her sides other ships would always give her a wide berth where possible. As she sailed through the Gulf of Oman before turning sharply right past Al Hadd - the easternmost point of Oman she set course for the Archipel des Comores an island archipelago between Mozambique and Madagascar over 2,000 nautical miles away. Her rhumb line course took her only fifty miles east of Socotra - well within the range of its powerful sea radars - and shortly after she was detected encrypted radio messages were passed to various listening stations in Yemen and Somalia.

Ten hours later a seventy-foot 'mother ship' said goodbye to two twenty-foot skiffs, both fitted with powerful twin outboards giving a speed of over thirty-five knots and each armed with six pirates. Although the *Methane Queen* was also equipped with the standard anti-hijacking system of high-powered water hoses, she did not have armed guards on board. As the pirates approached the ship, the pirate leader radioed and ordered the *Methane Queen* to slow engines. The captain of the *'Queen* did all he could. He increased engine speed, turned port and starboard to ward off close approach, and activated the water hoses. Increasing speed and getting in close to within 100 metres, the pirate leader fired a volley of shots into the bridge windows before demanding the hoses were turned off, or they would stand off and begin shooting with rifles and RPG's. With little choice, the captain was forced to agree and instructed the hoses turned off and the engines slowed. But not before radioing an emergency on the international distress frequency of 2182 kHz, and pressing the emergency buttons on the Digital Selective Calling system (DSC), and the Global Maritime Distress and Safety Systems (GMDSS). He also managed to call the Qatar Gas headquarters by satellite radio and declared their hijacking before alerting his small group of 20 crew to the impending takeover.

The DSC and GMDSS signals were immediately picked up by various craft within a thousand mile radius, including the Oman radar site at Jebel al Harim, which oversees the Straits of Hormuz shipping channel. Radio operators aboard various ships within the U.S. Fifth Fleet Carrier Battle Group steaming north through the Arabian Sea also intercepted the messages and passed them on to their captains and up the chain to Washington.

8

Eight minutes after the alarm had been sounded Deacon received a call in his barracks at Camp Lemonnier ordering him and his men to immediate action. Racing over to the control room he received the latest updates on the situation. Connecting by voice and video back to Coronado, his commanding officer, Rear-Admiral Lowe, came on the line.

"Lieutenant, we need you and your team to secure the *Methane Queen*. Two F/A 18 Super Hornets are on their way from the 'Truman with orders to stop anyone else approaching the *'Queen*.

You need to find a way to get on board, eliminate the pirates and free the ship. The deck of the *'Queen* isn't conducive to a parachute landing so you may need to go for a 'copter insertion. I'll leave that up to you. I want your attack plan within the hour."

Twenty minutes later Deacon was in contact with the commander of the aircraft carrier, the *USS Harry S. Truman.* The commander said, "Lieutenant, pilots have just completed a number of low-level flypasts of the *Methane Queen.* They report all deck lights are on and as soon as they approached they saw the pirates out along the decks firing weapons towards them. The captain of the *Methane,*

Captain Richard Fastman, then called us on 2182 stating we have to keep clear. The pirate leader, Mahmoud al-Afari, has locked all the crew, apart from Fastman and his helmsman, down below. Their room is wired with explosives, along with two of the LNG domes, and any approach by any ship or aircraft within two miles will result in him detonating the explosives. Fastman said this Afari is holding what looks to be a Deadman's radio switch in his hand. Afari is demanding a payment of US$400 million, or he will detonate the explosives and kill everyone on board. I've ordered the pilots to standoff, but stay on station. Over to you, Lieutenant."

Deacon rubbed the back of his neck and thought 'Fuck it'. There are only two main ways to get on board a moving ship. Either from another vessel such as a ship or launch or from the air by helicopter or parachute. Any method can be observed if someone is looking for it and although boarding can be quick, it can't be as fast as someone pressing a bomb trigger, especially if they are detected approaching, and it becomes a firefight. Also, having any sort of firefight on board a pressurised floating bomb with the power of a small nuke that could be triggered by a single stray bullet was not a very sound plan. Given enough time he could come up with a boarding plan using a submersible, especially after the 'Queen reached her destination and was at anchor.

However, the nearest suitable submersible was days away. Moreover, once the vessel was anchored the crew would be taken ashore and guarded. No, he had to think of a plan to free the hostages and the ship before it reached its final anchorage.

He sat down, closed his eyes and thought. He'd always found the best way to really concentrate on something was to remove all outside distractions, close himself off and just think about the task at hand.

Ten minutes later it came to him. He called Admiral Lowe back and explained his plan in detail. It wasn't the best plan he'd ever had, but it was the best one possible with the current limitations both in time and location. Lowe listened, asked a few questions, then finished by saying, "You, Lieutenant, are one crazy SoB, but I approve. Good luck. You'll need it."

The C-130 took off two hours later. On board, apart from the aircraft crew, were Deacon and his team, along with three black inflatable dinghies, two with electric motors fitted, several holdalls and a large plastic container strapped to the third dinghy. Ninety minutes later saw them approaching close to the *Methane Queen's* planned route. Deacon had already confirmed from the aircraft watching the *'Queen* that she was still maintaining the same course and speed. Twenty knots equates to one nautical mile every three minutes, so Deacon ordered the pilot of the C-130 to fly their intercept course fifteen miles in front of the *'Queen's* current position, or forty-five minutes steaming time away.

Deacon was nervous. They'd discussed this insertion method back in Coronado and had trialled it a number of times, but always using helicopters. Trying to achieve the same results from a C-130, even flying as slowly as 130 mph, was an enormous challenge. Unfortunately, the distance from Djibouti and the speed required to commence the rescue left little other option.

A few minutes later flying at the height of 300 feet and with an airspeed of 130 mph, the C-130 with all navigation lights extinguished crossed fifteen miles directly in front of the *Methane Queen's* tracked path. From that distance, the hijackers on board the 'Queen could neither see nor hear the engines of the C-130. Travelling at an airspeed of 190 feet per second, Deacon and his team had only two seconds to deploy men and equipment. One-half second after exiting the aircraft, the parachutes attached to the men and dinghies automatically deployed and four seconds later they hit the water, their parachutes hardly having time to fill and slow their descent and forward speed.

Virtually knocked unconscious by the impact from the sea, their dark-coloured automatic lifejackets automatically inflated and kept them on the surface, while the initial numbing shock of impact on their bodies slowly wore off. Drogues automatically deployed from the bottom of the dinghies to keep them from drifting.

"Forty-three minutes. C'mon, let's move" Deacon said groggily through the waterproof microphone comms system, trying to bring life back into his battered limbs. Climbing as quickly as their bodies would allow, O'Flannigan and Deacon slowly climbed into one of the two motorised dinghies, while Hymann and Schaefer clambered into the other.

Once in and secure, they hauled the third dinghy towards them and seized the loose ends of the large cable drum.

After tying off an end each, Deacon nodded at Hymann who stuck the tip of his Ka-BAR into each inflated tube of the third dinghy and it began to slowly deflate, air hissing noisily through the small cuts. The electric motors took a slight strain, and both dinghies began pulling away as the cable unravelled from the drum on the slowly sinking third inflatable. The cable, a mixture of polypropylene to float and Kevlar for strength, unravelled equally in both directions and floated on the water. As the reel neared the end of its 600 metres length, the dinghy supporting its weight finally sank, and the two towing dinghies pulled the remaining cable taut.

"Nine minutes to go. Clear port light."

"Clear starboard light," came the reply from 600 metres away and Deacon finally breathed a sigh of relief. This complete operation bordered on two unknowns. Could they land safely from a moving C-130 and carry out this task as easily as a helicopter dropping them in the correct position; and would the approaching ship stay on the same course thereby allowing them to get into position.

At each half-minute interval, they counted off the view of the port and starboard lights still showing clearly amongst the bright deck lights. As long as the *'Queen* didn't turn they were happy.

At ten seconds after the expected contact, O'Flannigan and Hymann, with hands on the connecting cable, both reported they felt the 'schnick' as the bow of the *'Queen* caught the floating cable.

As the *Methane Queen* steamed ahead, the captured cable pulled taut and both dinghies, one on either side, began to move together and forward. Within minutes, both dinghies were close together seventy metres or so behind the stern of the *'Queen*, being pulled along at 20 knots. The port dinghy with Schaefer and Hymann in was slightly in front due to the *'Queen* catching the cable slightly off-centre. The two dinghies were now being pulled being the *'Queen* in its white, frothy wake which presented its own problems. The wake of a ship is caused by the pressure differences of the hull through water and the churning and aeration by the propellers, or screws. Unfortunately, aerated seawater does not contain as much buoyancy as normal seawater, and the churning effect could suck anything floating down beneath the surface, even the inflatable dinghies. Also, anyone on board the *'Queen* looking astern might see the two dark dinghies against the white froth of the wake.

With their rucksacks in place, weapons securely fastened over their shoulders, night-vision goggles in place, and short water skis on their feet, Deacon issued the order. Each SEAL clipped their ski rope handle and tow rope onto the cable with a small device and surged forward. Within seconds, all four men were water-skiing in the wake behind the *'Queen* as the dinghies, now freed, bobbed away into the distance to be picked up later by a patrolling helicopter from the Fifth Fleet which would home in on their radio beacons. Each SEAL also carried the same radio beacon in the event they fell, and would be picked up later.

9

Like a scene from a James Bond movie, all four SEALs slowly advanced towards the stern of the *Methane Queen*, the small devices on each towrope slowly moving them forward. The smooth frothy wake surface made the skiing relatively easy, and the four figures were too small to be seen amongst the froth if anyone happened to look from the stern. It took the SEALs almost fifteen minutes to get close into the stern of the *'Queen*, the small devices working flawlessly gripping and pulling them forward. Through their goggles, they could see there were no hijackers in sight anywhere near the stern. Apparently, the leader of the group, Mahmoud al-Afari, was not expecting anyone coming up from the rear without being seen on radar. He had stationed two men, one on each bridge wing, to keep an eye out for helicopters, but had relied on the ship's radar to detect anything floating. However, the error he'd made was in overestimating the ability of the marine radar systems. These are very sophisticated radars, designed to show large and small craft and vessel track movement, as well as displaying rain and, naturally, land itself. The echoes returned from the rubber dinghies, even with the small electric motors attached, were not large enough to escape from the 'clutter' each wave typically returns and is automatically filtered out by the excellent software.

Now as they approached, each SEAL using his free hand over his shoulder, manhandled what looked to be a large pistol out of his rucksack. The pistol was actually a gas gun loaded with a small five-prong rubber-coated carbon fibre grappling hook and cable. To get a clear view of the stern railing each SEAL had to lean back as far as possible, take his eyes off the rear of the ship or the water, sight and aim the gas gun and fire. As Hymann leant back, his right water ski dug into a small wave and twisted him. Unable to turn back in time, the ski caught the 20-knot force of the water rushing past and was ripped off his foot.

With only one ski remaining, Hymann was unbalanced and fell into the churning froth disappearing immediately from view.

The immediate worry for Deacon was the closeness of the ships screws and that Hymann might be pulled into them, but the speed of the ship just caused him to tumble over and over to a depth of almost forty feet before slowly resurfacing over one hundred feet astern. "Sorry boss, I snafu'd that. Good luck, see you back at base," he radioed as the ship steamed on. He activated his radio beacon and relaxed, floating on the surface to await the helicopter pick up in an hour or so.

In the meantime, O'Flannigan and Schaefer had managed their balancing act, and both their grapple hooks had landed almost silently across the ship's rail; carbon fibre being lighter than steel, but many times as strong and quieter in its landing.

Deacon turned, leant back, aimed and fired in one smooth movement, his hook finding company amongst the other two. Kicking off their skis, all three rappelled hand-over-hand up and 'walked' up the vertical metal stern of the *'Queen* before stopping just below deck level, their rubber boots efficiently helping grip the steel hull. Easing their heads up slowly to deck level, they looked around to see if anyone was near.

The bright deck lights clearly illuminated the ship but removed the advantages the SEALs normally had of working in the dark. Although any pirates would be clearly visible, so would Deacon and his team.

As they'd climbed they lost sight of the two pirates stationed at either end of the bridge wing, but in turn, they couldn't now see the SEALs. Schaefer thought he could see movement almost halfway along the starboard side of the ship, and when the figure disappeared all three of them quickly climbed over the stern railings and moved into the shadows below the Boat Deck level of the superstructure. Above that was the Bridge Deck, then the High Bridge

Deck, and finally, the Wheel Bridge Deck where the captain and the pirate leader were likely to be. The captain, Richard Fastman, had said the pirates had locked all his crew down below. Deacon didn't know for sure where, but it was likely to be in the main mess hall on the Bridge Deck.

What worried Deacon more were the explosives the pirate leader had planted. Even one small explosion would be enough to trigger the liquid propane and turn the entire ship into a gigantic bomb. Moving silently up one set of stairs and along the corridors, suppressed rifles at the ready, the team approached the mess hall. With a faint smell of cigarette smoke hanging in the air, Schaefer looked around the corner using a micro-thin endoscope connected to a small screen. The endoscope flexible probe end was only slightly larger than a match head, but its wide-angled lens gave a clear view of the corridor.

Two guards were standing leaning against the metals walls. Both were smoking vile smelling cigarettes, and one was speaking. He had his rifle loosely held leaning against his shoulder while the other had placed his weapon on a chair. The fact they were smoking and had a naked flame on a floating bomb needing just one spark to set off a chain reaction seemed to escape them, or maybe they didn't care.

With weapons ready, Deacon counted to three, and they walked around the corner. His movement caused both pirates to jump and look at him. In the tenth of a second it took to register in their brains that a figure of a man, dressed in black Nomex, and carrying a rifle was looking at them, Schaefer and O'Flannigan sighted their green lasers onto their centre body masses and each fired three times. The suppressed rounds made the faintest of pops, and both pirates were dead before they could even raise a shout, their cigarettes slipping from their fingers. The one holding his rifle just slumped backwards and slid down the wall while the other was thrown back by the force of the rounds entering his chest and fell over the chair with a crash.

Deacon and O'Flannigan rushed to the door in case there were other pirates inside about to come out to investigate the noise, while Schafer stood guard in the corridor.

Testing the door handle very carefully, O'Flannigan murmured, "It's locked."

Deacon checked both bodies and found the key in the second's pirates clothes. Quietly inserting it into the lock, O'Flannigan slowly turned the handle. Both men had their Sig-Sauer suppressed pistols at the ready as O'Flannigan suddenly swung the door wide and dived in.

10

The surprised and startled looks on the fifteen men's faces said it all. Although the clatter of the guard falling over the chair had sounded loud in the corridor, the thick doors had insulated the sounds to those inside. Both SEALs raised fingers to their lips for silence as they rapidly scanned the room for any attackers. Realising they were amongst friends, Deacon called Schaefer over his radio, and together they dragged the dead bodies into the room and out of sight.

One of the older prisoners stood, saying, "Well whoever you are, welcome. I'm Chief Officer Andy Birkstorm."

"Chief, I'm Lieutenant Deacon, and we're the U.S. Navy here to get you out. How many attackers are there and how many hostages?"

"Well, Lieutenant, you sure are a sight for sore eyes. Unless more have joined, there are ten pirates, minus the two dead ones here. As for us, there is twenty crew in total. Fifteen of us are here, with the captain and helmsman still on the bridge. The Chief Engineer and his second are still in the engine room with at least one guard - that makes nineteen - and Pav Nguyen, the Second Officer is out checking on the refrigeration systems. That's his area of expertise, and I saw one guard with him as we were brought down here. The pirate leader ordered two of his men to go forward and be lookouts, but I don't know where the rest are."

Schaefer said, "Boss, we've got two dead here, two are on the bridge wings, that's four. Say two as forward lookouts, one with this guy Nguyen, and one in the engine room. That leaves two on the bridge including the leader, this al-Afari guy".

"The other problem Lieutenant," Birkstorm continued, "is the bastards placed explosives. I was up on the bridge with the captain when we got taken. They were going to rig this room, but I don't think they had enough, so they moved the rest of the crew down here and put guards outside instead. But two of them each with a satchel went down amongst the domes for about twenty minutes. They didn't have the satchels with them when they got back, and after talking to the leader, he got a device out of his pocket and pressed a button. It beeped three times, and he smiled and said something to his men. They then decided to keep just the captain and helmsman on the bridge, and I was brought down here, but I heard the leader telling the captain that the ship is rigged and he would detonate it if any rescue attempts are made."

"Did you hear anything else?"

"No, Lieutenant, I was too far away and on my way down here. The guards didn't speak any English to us only Arabic or something to each other."

"Somali, not Arabic, I think," Deacon replied. "Did you see where they placed the explosives?"

"The 'Queen has nine pressure domes, or tanks, set in three sets of three. They placed the explosives on domes two, five, and eight, the central dome of each group. Just one dome going up would take the rest with it. At minus 260C and 600 to 1 pressure, you don't need much of a bang to start something. Just releasing the gas into the atmosphere would cause it to explode due to the temperature difference. With everything running normally, it's as safe as possible. But basically, we are floating on a powered raft with nine highly unstable small nuclear devices on board."

Deacon stood there thinking for a few minutes before turning to Schaefer, O'Flannigan, and Birkstorm. "Chief, get your best man to go with Flan here. Flan, you go and take out the guard in the engine room. I don't want any disruption to alert the bridge. Same speed etc. As soon as the threat is eliminated, get the engineer to be ready to switch off all the lights. He might have to take the generator offline. Whatever. On my command, I want all the lights out. Then get your ass up to the High

Bridge Deck. Bryant, you go on ahead to the same deck and check it out. You should be able to climb from there to the Wheel Bridge Deck when Flan's back with you and get into position to take out both bridge wing pirates. On my second command, you do that then storm the bridge wheelhouse itself and take out al-Afari and his colleague."

Schaefer looked a little bemused, "So where will you be, boss?"

"Chief Birkstorm and I need to go and eliminate the two lookouts and the guy guarding Pav Nguyen. If they raise the alarm, al-Afari will likely detonate the *'Queen* and even if they fight back, a single stray round hitting any one of the nine tanks ... Well, let's just say we'll be back at base before the C-130."

"What about the explosives? What if we don't get al-Afari in time and he detonates?"

"That's why I'm gonna have Chief Birkstorm with me. After I eliminate the targets, I'll be in bomb disposal mode. The Chief can guide me around. As soon as they are all neutralised, I'll give the command to eliminate the bridge wing guards."

"And if we're discovered before, or if the lights out spooks al-Afari to detonating?"

"Al-Afari has to be neutralised and the trigger secured. That's the primary objective. But I don't think he will do anything when the lights fail. He'll panic and try and contact his men, but he won't reach any. He'll assume it's a technical problem, and he'll shout and scream, but he won't chance losing the *'Queen* until he's sure he's about to lose. We'll be done before that. C'mom, let's go."

Telling the remaining hostages to stay together and wait in the mess hall, Deacon led his men out accompanied by Chief Birkstorm and Able Seaman Brad Cummings.

Schaefer headed up the outside stairs carefully to watch and get the best position while Brad Cummings led O'Flannigan down towards the engine room. Deacon and Birkstorm edged into the shadows and advanced slowly along the port side of the ship.

After dropping down the equivalent of five floors and moving forward almost a third of the ship's length, Cummings and O'Flannigan came to the engine room entrance. Leaving Cummings outside, O'Flannigan crept quietly forward until he could see the three men below. The guard was waving his AK-47 towards both of the crew and shouting in Somali. The two engineers couldn't understand him, but Deacon guessed this hadn't stopped the pirate from beating one of them. The older crew member, who O'Flannigan assumed to be the Chief Engineer, had dried blood covering much of his face and his clothes looked ripped. It seemed like either he hadn't obeyed orders quickly enough to stave off a beating, or maybe the pirate was sadistic and just liked giving pain. Either way, O'Flannigan reckoned, the pirate was going to get what he deserved.

Tiptoeing back outside, he spoke with Cummings, "Brad, from the entrance I can't get a clean shot without him seeing me. I need you to go in and give yourself up over towards the other side of the engine room. As soon as he sees you and turns, I can get into position and nail the bastard. You up for that?"

Nodding nervously, Brad Cummings agreed to go to the other entrance door. O'Flannigan stayed just inside the engine room door, hidden entirely in the shadows until he saw the opposite door open. Brad Cummings entered, and called out 'Hello'. The guard spun around and raised his weapon, shouting in Somali at Brad to come and get down on the floor. He was just reaching for his radio to call al-Afari when three rapid suppressed shots sounded softly amongst the steel of the ship's powerhouse and pirate number three joined his two other colleagues in 'Jannah', the Muslim equivalent of Heaven.

After speaking with the two engineers and making sure the older guy's injuries weren't serious, the senior engineer led O'Flannigan to the auxiliary power generator, having started the shutdown procedure of the primary one.

"When you press that button, the lights will go out within about three seconds. I've switched off the primary generator and disabled the alarm up to the bridge. It's all running on this auxiliary unit and pressing that button will kill it," the Chief Engineer said.

O'Flannigan stood there waiting for Deacon's command before hightailing it back up on deck and on up to find Schaefer.

Schaefer, meanwhile, had silently climbed up to the High Bridge Deck, the level immediately below the Wheel Bridge Deck with its bridge wings extending out either side, over the edges of the ship. He took the port aspect, having already agreed O'Flannigan would take the starboard.

From here, sat in the shadows, he had a clear view of his lookouts and knew O'Flannigan would do the same. They would wait for Deacon's command then eliminate the lookouts before storming the wheelhouse moments later, just fourteen metals steps above where they were hidden.

11

After leaving the mess hall, Deacon and Birkstorm had crept quietly into the shadows outside and began to move slowly along the port side of the ship. The blaze of lights would hamper their movements as anyone in the wheelhouse looking down and either bridge wing lookout looking forward would have a clear illuminated view of them.

On any ship, there are nooks and places where off-duty seamen will go for a little peace and quiet away from colleagues when at sea. Most would be hidden from view directly from the bridge. Deacon's reason for taking

Birkstorm was his knowledge of these spots possibly having found and used some himself over the years.

At two-hundred-and-twenty-five metres length from stem to stern, the *Methane Queen* was by no means a small ship. Even walking at an average pace would take them a few minutes to travel its length, but to do so covertly took many more. The first person they saw was Pav Nguyen working near the central pressurised refrigeration unit. The guard with him was leaning against the metal superstructure, his weapon slung over his shoulder. They had been here doing the rounds across the various refrigeration units for hours, and he was bored senseless beyond belief. He, like the other pirates, was also chewing Khat, the herbal stimulant prevalent throughout this region of Africa, but banned in most western countries. Although his senses were stimulated by his constant chewing, the secondary effect of Khat was in slowing reaction times.

Not wanting to risk a shot in the close confines of the pressurised tanks Deacon merely stepped out from what little shadow there was, looked straight at him and said 'Boo'.

In his stimulated condition the pirate saw the movement of a figure in front of him, heard the word 'Boo', but his arms felt like lead.

Before he could raise his arms or even try to slip his rifle off his shoulder Deacon was on him. With a quick movement, Deacon thrust the 9-inch blade of his Ka-BAR knife into the soft tissues of his upper stomach and up into his lungs and heart. The razor sharp blade sliced easily through soft skin and muscle as Deacon placed a hand over the pirate's mouth to stop him crying out.

With a final extra thrust Deacon drove the blade in deeper, the sharpened tip slicing the heart in half, and with a final sigh, the pirate collapsed onto the steel deck.

"Four down, six to go," he radioed, before looking around into the frightened eyes of Pav Nguyen. Luckily, before

Nguyen could panic and run, Chief Birkstorm placed a hand on his shoulder and said, "Your safe now son. Thank the nice Lieutenant for saving your life."

Shaking with nerves, Pav extended a hand and Deacon shook it warmly.

"Do you know where the explosives are placed?"

"Yes, yes I do, Lieutenant. They are on the middle tanks of all three sections. On tanks two, five and eight. All near the top."

"And is the explosives still in the satchels?"

"No, they removed them and pressed them onto the tanks by the pipes. They each have something plastic sticking out with an aerial attached and a flashing light."

Cursing quietly as the job had just got harder and wishing he had the extra manpower of Bill Hymann, he finally said into his radio, "Flan, Bryant. I'm gonna take out the bow lookouts and pass their radios to Birkstorm and Nguyen. When the lights go out, and al-Afari starts shouting I'll get these two to keep shouting 'Allahu Ackbar' for a few minutes. That'll hopefully confuse al-Afari and buy us some time."

Moving a little more freely forward now as the front half of the ship offered better cover from being seen from the bridge region, Deacon quickly spied the forward lookouts leaning against the handrail, close to the bow. Both seemed bored, were chewing Khat, and one was holding his AK-47 loosely by the barrel. The other had his weapon slung over a shoulder. However, they also had what looked to be RPG launchers near their feet.

Sighting on the body mass of the first, Deacon fired a burst of three rounds stitching a short line across his chest. The suppressed pops were carried away by the wind, and the other pirate didn't even notice, but he did hear the AK-47 fall and land on the steel deck. He turned at the sound, and although he saw his colleague lying on the floor with blood oozing around him, his Khat drugged brain was slow to react. By the time he'd even thought of raising his rifle Deacon's next burst of three rounds had cleaved his chest in two.

Rushing over and dragging both bodies out of sight, Deacon retrieved their radios and passed them to Birkstorm and Nguyen.

"When the lights go out, and you hear al-Afari yelling into the radio, start Allahu Akbar 'ing down these. In fact, shout any Arabic or Somali words you can think of."

Grabbing the shirt off one of the dead pirates, Deacon pulled it over his dark Nomex suit.

"If anyone sees me from the bridge, they might think it's one of them and not open fire," he said to the quizzed looks from Birkstorm and Nguyen.

The pressure domes and tanks were numbered one through nine from bow to stern of the *'Queen,* so Deacon moved aft towards tank number two.

Approaching from the bow direction would keep most of Deacon out of site that far from the bridge as he climbed up on top of the dome. It was smooth shiny polished steel and slippery. He slid forward as much as possible on his stomach, grateful this time for the deck lights making it easy for him to see the set-up. To save slipping down off the tank he had to place one arm around the central pipe.

The pirates were using plastic explosives and had moulded it around the base of the main pipe entering the dome directly from on top. Placed into the explosive were two small metal tubes with wires attached. These were the detonators and were connected to a plastic box with an aerial and a pulsing red lamp attached. The plastic explosives on their own were pretty harmless without the detonators to trigger them. Reaching up, Deacon could just reach the two detonators and managed to pull them free before cutting the wires with his knife.

With the detonators removed, the plastic explosive was now harmless. Unfortunately, the plastic box had a simple anti-tamper device fitted, and the cutting of the detonator cables had triggered an alarm. The pulsing red lamp on the plastic box went out, and the unit sent a radio signal back to its control indicating it had lost connections.

The Deadman's switch in al-Afari's hand beeped three times and then began flashing.

Al-Afari grabbed binoculars and looked forward almost 170 metres from the bridge to see what looked like one of his men climbing down from pressure dome number two. He grabbed the radio and started shouting into it, rushing out onto one of the bridge wings for a better view. Still screaming into his radio suddenly the ship's lights went out, and with his eyes still accustomed to the brightness of the white decks and superstructure, he suddenly couldn't see a thing.

12

As soon as he'd seen the pulsing red light extinguish on the plastic box, Deacon guessed what had happened. As the radios in the hands of Birkstorm and Nguyen started squawking, he thumped his radio mic switch and said, "Lights down now. Kill the lights."

Two heartbeats later, the ship was plunged into darkness. In the sudden darkness, it was disorienting, but Deacon pulled his night vision goggles down over his eyes and switched them on.

He heard Schaefer report that he had one bridge wing pirate in his sights and he could still hear Birkstorm and Nguyen shouting various Arabic sounding words into the radios. He guessed that O'Flannigan would be part way up inside the bridge superstructure now, but they'd need to wait until O'Flannigan was also in position before he could risk them attacking the wheelhouse.

It took Deacon less than a minute to get to dome number five. He scrambled up the steps and crawled out onto the top of the slippery dome, faster now as there was no need to try and stay hidden. The green glow of his NVG's making it almost as bright as before. Pulling both detonators out of the explosives, he again cut their wires before dropping them on the deck, the pulsing red light on the attached box suddenly stopping flashing.

Sliding down onto the steps he ran back down to the deck as fast as he could, not seeing the edge of a gate flange in front of him. He fell heavily and the sharp metal sliced through his Nomex suit cutting into his right calf muscle deeply.

Cursing he half-ran, half-hobbled towards the last set of three domes. These, being closer to the rear of the ship and almost touching the bridge superstructure were a slightly different shape.

Climbing the steps of dome eight he could see the tops of these three domes was steeper than the others. Looking down he saw the pirates had used a rope to pull themselves up to the pipe connection, but Deacon realised there wasn't time to do this now. Climbing onto the handrail of the steps, he leapt as high onto the dome roof as he could, his rubber boots scrabbling for grip and a toe-hold. He found by spreading his arms wide and hugging the dome roof, he could slowly push himself up towards the peak by using his toes, but leaving a bloody trail from his injured leg behind him.

His radio squawked, "Boss, I can hear al-Afari shouting to his men. I think they're gonna start firing any moment," Schaefer said.

Before he could respond, a powerful flashlight beamed down on him temporarily blinding him. His NVG's amplified the intense light by twenty thousand times and intense pain raced from his optic nerves to deep within his brain.

"Take 'em out. Take out the bridge guards and capture the bridge," he shouted into the microphone just as his outstretched hand managed to touch the central pipe.

As he tried to extend his fingers around the pipe so to pull himself up, the wheelhouse windows above exploded in a mass of bullets as glass rained down on him.

Finally, his luck ran out, and the toes of his right boot began slipping in the blood trail, and he felt himself start sliding down the dome; the red light on the explosive package still attached to the central pipe flashing ominously.

13

Bryant Schaefer had been biding his time. He'd had the lookout pirate in his sights out towards the port wing almost the whole time, just waiting for the lights to be extinguished, and for O'Flannigan to get into position on the starboard side. Twice al-Afari had walked out onto the wing, but Schaefer couldn't risk a shot until Deacon had confirmed the explosives were neutralised. A Deadman's switch was just that. While alive, your hand or finger kept the spring-loaded trigger compressed. If you dropped it or suddenly died, the switch would fall from your hand, and the trigger would release. You couldn't even try shooting it out of someone's hand, thinking if you smash the radio part then it couldn't trigger - only the simplest of ones worked that way. Anything more advanced would be in constant synchronised communication with the detonators on the explosives. If the radio link should fail by being jammed, or the Deadman's switch triggered or destroyed, the explosives would immediately be detonated.

The only safe method was to disconnect the detonators and remove them from the explosives so all Schaefer could do was wait.

After what seemed an age, there was suddenly shouting and activity inside the wheelhouse. Al-Afari was screaming into his radio and rushed out to the starboard bridge wing, looking forward towards the bow through binoculars. Schafer was just about to raise the alarm when Deacon's voice cut over the airwaves, "Lights down now. Kill the lights."

Moments later everything plunged into darkness, and he quickly slid his NVG's back over his eyes. He could still hear al-Afari shouting into his radio and demanding answers from his men.

The two bridge lookouts went rushing into the wheelhouse, and Schaefer could hear shouting and cursing. Both reappeared a few minutes later and stood guard arguing and looking both forward and aft for any sign of movement. The one on the starboard bridge wing, out of shot angle from where Schaefer was hiding, picked something up and Schaefer radioed, "Boss, I can hear al-Afari shouting to his men. I think they're gonna start firing any moment," moments before the pirate turned on a large powerful torch and shone it done onto the deck area below.

With most surprise lost, Schaefer did what he thought best. He re-aimed for the guard he could see, fired three times, and raced for the stairs that would take him to the wheelhouse as he saw his target collapse.

O'Flannigan had managed the climb from the engine room to the High Bridge Deck in record time. Hearing Deacon's radio shout he rushed up the last few stairs, quickly sighted on the pirate with the torch and fired. Only one of his rounds found its target, and the pirate slumped, dropping the torch. As he turned and tried to raise his AK-47, O'Flannigan fired another three times, this time all on target, before running up the stairs to the wheelhouse.

Schaefer burst into the port side of the wheelhouse. What was presented to him was the helmsman leaning against the wheel, dried blood across his face and head, with a guard stood immediately behind. Captain Fastman was sat in the corner slumped on the floor. He'd been beaten, and his white shirt was stained crimson with blood.

Three of the fingers on his left hand were sticking out sideways, his eyes looked blackened, and his foot was sticking at a strange angle. Near to the captain the leader of the pirates, Mahmoud al-Afari, was standing holding the Deadman's switch and pointing a handgun at the captain's head.

As the guard near the helmsman turned to aim initially at Schaefer, O'Flannigan burst in and pulled the trigger, his three-round burst hitting the pirate in the throat and chest. As the pirate fell, his fingers locked and his weapon sprayed rounds across the ceiling of the wheelhouse and out through the front windows, spraying glass all around.

The pirate leader had his weapon against the captain's temple. He said, "You're too late," holding the Deadman's switch in close to his body.

The first bullet of Schaefer's three-round burst caught him high in the cheek, shattering his eye socket, before exiting near his ear. The second caught him just below his other ear and exited with parts of his spinal column. The third took the top third of his skull with it.

As the Deadman's switch fell from his now dead hand, the trigger released and the communications between the trigger and the receiver caused a voltage to trigger the two detonators connected to it.

One-tenth of a second later a bright flash lit up the wheelhouse, and the sounds of a loud 'boom' echoed around the room.

14

Rushing to the broken windows to look down Schaefer yelled into his radio, "Boss, Boss, JOHN!"

As the cloud of black smoke drifted away, the radio crackled, and a voice said, "First beer's on you."

Ten minutes later, with the ship's doctor checking over the captain, Lieutenant John Deacon walked limping slightly onto the bridge, saluted and extended his hand. "Captain Fastman, I'm pleased to say the ship is yours."

Grasping Deacon's hand with his one good one, Fastman looked Deacon in the eye and said, "How the hell did you get aboard? How come we're all still alive?"

"Captain, getting aboard was easy. We just swam fast."

Seeing the bemused look on Fastman's face, Deacon continued, "We actually lassoed the ship. We placed a line across the water in front of your course. The bow snagged it and pulled us in close behind. The pirates were looking out expected a helicopter or boat attack, not swimmers."

"But what if the *'Queen* had missed or the cable had gone down under the keel?"

"Well, the *'Queen* hadn't changed course for over five hours, so it was pretty likely to stay on course. As for the keel, there wasn't any worry over that. The 'Queen has a bow bulb. Once the cable was snagged, it was there to stay."

"But what about the explosives. I heard an explosion."

"Well I'd managed to defuse the explosives on tanks two and five, but then got a bit stuck on tank eight just forward here. I'd cut my leg and began sliding back down the dome when my colleagues here entered the wheelhouse. The receiver was still connected to the detonators in the plastic explosives, and I couldn't remove them in time. When I started slipping, I knew I only had one chance. I lunged and ripped the receiver off the pipe, along with the detonators still attached. When the pirate leader was shot and the switch triggered, the detonators exploded, but one of them must have had a little bit of explosive stuck to it. Luckily, by that time I was fast sliding off the dome and onto the railings. I was still holding them, and the flash and bang were the detonators exploding, but they were too far away from the other plastic explosives to cause a problem. They gave me a bit of a shock, and my ears are still ringing, but it's all safe now. We'll scrape the rest of the plastic explosive off the domes and drop it in the ocean. It's harmless without a detonator."

"Lieutenant, I don't know how my crew and I can ever thank you and your men."

"All in a day's work, Captain. Now turn us around and let's get the hell away from here. We'll be meeting up with a destroyer from the Fifth Fleet sometime later this morning. In the meantime, can you get your cook to rustle us up some breakfast? I'm starving!"

Three hours later the *USS Momsen* steamed into view and took station one mile off the starboard side.

One thing the *Methane Queen* had in abundance on board were refrigerators. The pirates' bodies were already in cold storage for delivery and identification in the USA.

Deacon and his team climbed from the boarding ladder on the *'Queen* into a large waiting inflatable that whisked them back to the *Momsen*. A small group of marines would stay aboard the *'Queen* until she was clear of Tanzania, while a Naval Lieutenant had been placed in overall charge of the *'Queen* while Captain Fastman was airlifted for medical treatment and a replacement captain could be flown to join the ship at Cape Town.

With a last handshake with Captain Fastman on his way to the sickbay, Deacon turned and smiled as Bill Hymann walked in and apologised for his early swim.

The End

Mike Boshier

Other Books & Further Details

The Jaws of Revenge

After the capture and execution of Osama bin Laden, there is hope in the West Al-Qaeda will collapse. But with a brotherhood that has spanned over 1,000 years, the fight is bigger than one man. When good fortune smiles on the new leaders, they'd be fools not to grasp the opportunity. Enemies can become half friends when the prize is so big... In an audacious and terrifying plot to destroy America once and for all, teams are sent out to wreak havoc. One team of US SEALs stand in their way. One team of US SEALs can save America and the West. But time is running out. Will they be too late?

Terror of the Innocent

Join US Navy SEAL John Deacon as he stumbles across an ISIS revenge plot using deadly weapons stolen from Saddam's regime. Masterminded by Deacon's old adversary, Saif the Palestinian, and too late to save the UK, Deacon and the world can only watch in horror as thousands suffer a terrible fate. Determined to stop the same outcome in the US, Deacon is in a race against time.

Check out my web page www.mikeboshier.com for details of latest books, offers and free stuff.

About the Author

I am the author of the John Deacon series of action adventure novels. I make my online home at www.mikeboshier.com. You can connect with me on Twitter at https://twitter.com/MikeBoshier, on Facebook at www.facebook.com/AuthorMikeBoshier/ and you can send me an email at mike@mikeboshier.com if the mood strikes you.

Currently living in New Zealand, the books I enjoy reading are from great authors such as Andy McNab, David Baldacci, Brad Thor, Vince Flynn, Chris Ryan, etc. to name just a few. I've tried to write my books in a similar style. If you like adventure/thriller novels as I do, and you like the same authors as I do, then I hope you find mine do them justice.

www.mikeboshier.com

You Can Make a Big Difference

If you have enjoyed this book, it would be fantastic if you would consider sharing this message with others.

Thank you, Mike Boshier.

Other things you can do:

- Recommend this book to all your friends and colleagues.
- LIKE my Facebook Author page www.facebook.com/AuthorMike Boshier/and post a comment.
- Share as many times as you can on social media.

VIP Readers Mailing List

To join our VIP Readers Mailing List and receive updates about new books and freebies, please join my VIP Reader's List at www.mikeboshier.com.

I value your trust. Your email address will stay safe and you will never receive spam from me. You can unsubscribe at any time.

Thank you.

42214067R00087

Printed in Poland
by Amazon Fulfillment
Poland Sp. z o.o., Wrocław